For Pia and Izzy
And your great-grandmother, Alice.

www.enchantedlion.com

First edition published in 2025 by Enchanted Lion Books,
248 Creamer Street, Studio 4, Brooklyn, NY 11231
Text & illustrations copyright © 2025 by Giselle Potter
Book design by Emma Vitoria
All rights reserved under International
and Pan-American Copyright Conventions
A CIP record is on file with the Library of Congress
ISBN 978-1-59270-431-6
Printed in Italy by Società Editoriale Grafiche AZ
Distributed throughout the world by ABRAMS, New York

First Printing

The paintings in this book were created with watercolor on paper.

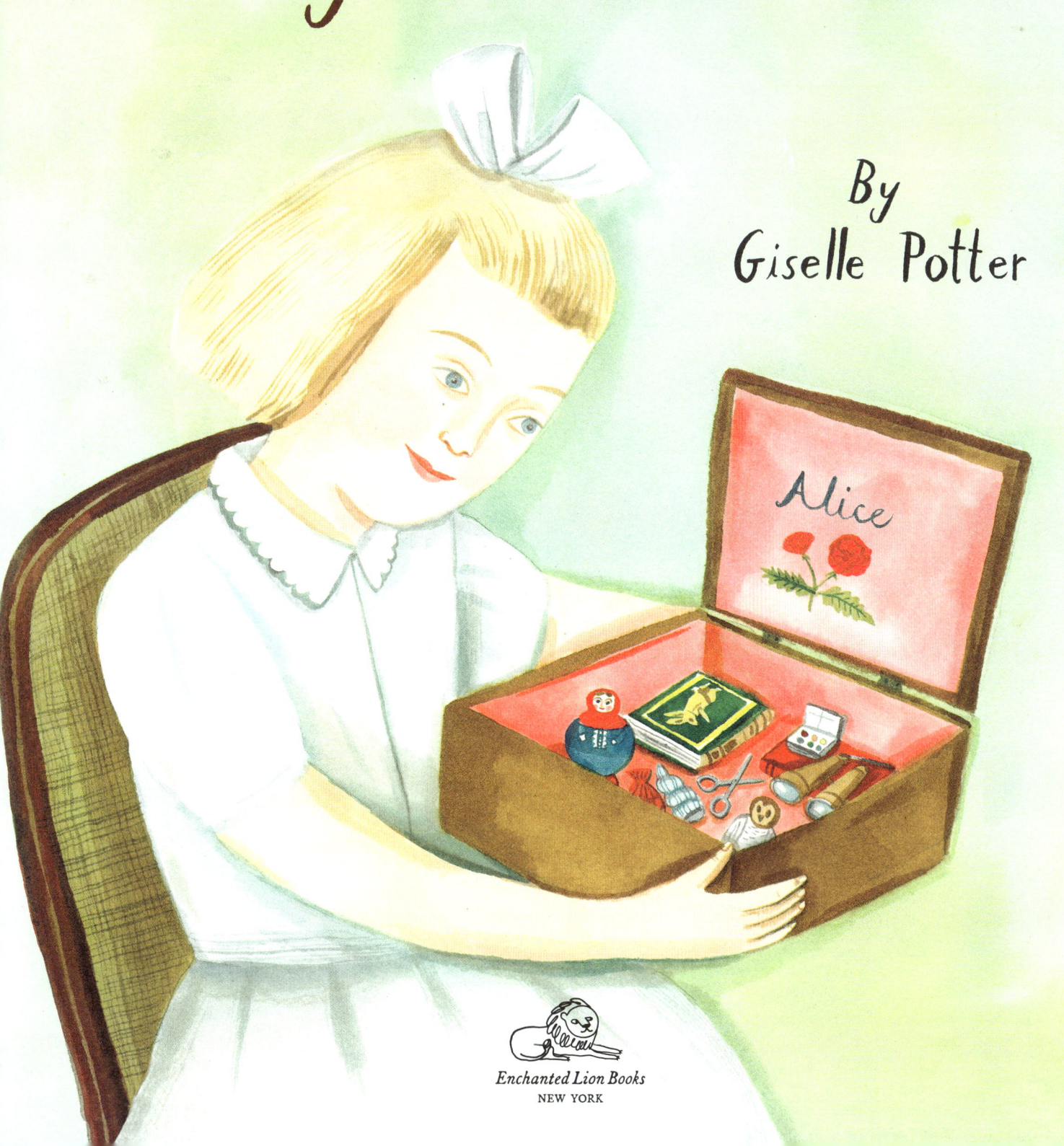

Before She Was My Grandmother

By
Giselle Potter

Enchanted Lion Books
NEW YORK

When I visit my grandmother, Alice, we sit together in her sunlit kitchen and tell each other stories.

She makes me feel important when she looks into my eyes and listens carefully to everything I have to say. She likes to hear all about my day, and she likes me to read to her.

But my favorite part is when she takes out
her box of special things:

her wooden stacking doll,
her copy of *Alice in Wonderland*,
a tiny watercolor set and small notebook,
her collection of stones and shells,
a pair of binoculars,
miniature scissors,
and her sisters' walnut owl.

Every object is a clue to a bigger story:
the story of her life before she was my grandmother.

Before she was my grandmother, Alice was a little girl born with stiff joints that kept her from running and playing like the other little girls. She often felt separate and alone, but that was a secret she kept to herself.

Her nurse gave her a small wooden doll. The doll's limbs were painted on and couldn't move, but you could open it up and find another doll inside… and then another.

Sometimes, Alice felt just like her wooden doll. Her body didn't move easily and there was more of her on the inside, because she filled her mind with every bit of knowledge she could find.

Her little sisters called her Queen Alice because she seemed so wise and regal, sitting above them on a mound, as they rolled and tumbled in the grass.

And while they splashed in the foamy sea, Alice would sit on the sand, collecting stones and shells.

Alice's days were spent reading and observing life. She knew the name of every flower in the garden and every bird that visited it, and she knew all their songs, too. She kept a little notebook with pressed flowers, and she painted pictures with her tiny watercolor set of the birds she saw.

Books carried her away on magical adventures. She especially liked *Alice in Wonderland*, because she liked to imagine she was also Alice, tumbling down her own rabbit hole into a different world.

At night, she often dreamt of a deer with legs like twigs and antlers that reached out and up into the clouds, higher than any tree. Flowers grew in its antlers and birds made nests there and sang their beautiful songs.

In the mornings, her sisters would curl up around her in bed, and she would tell them about her dreams.

One morning, sitting at the breakfast table, Alice felt the heavy stares of her parents. When her father cleared his throat, she tapped loudly at her egg with her spoon. She could already tell that she didn't want to hear what he had to say.

"Sweetheart, you'll be going away soon."

"To a lovely place in Switzerland, for little girls just like you," her mother quickly added.

All Alice could muster was a quiet, "Oh!"

She sat up straight in her chair with her bravest face, but inside she felt like melted ice cream at the thought of going far away and leaving her little sisters behind.

Soon, however, her mind started buzzing with images she remembered from books she had read of white-capped mountains, goats, and rosy-cheeked girls eating cheese, and she felt a burst of excitement.

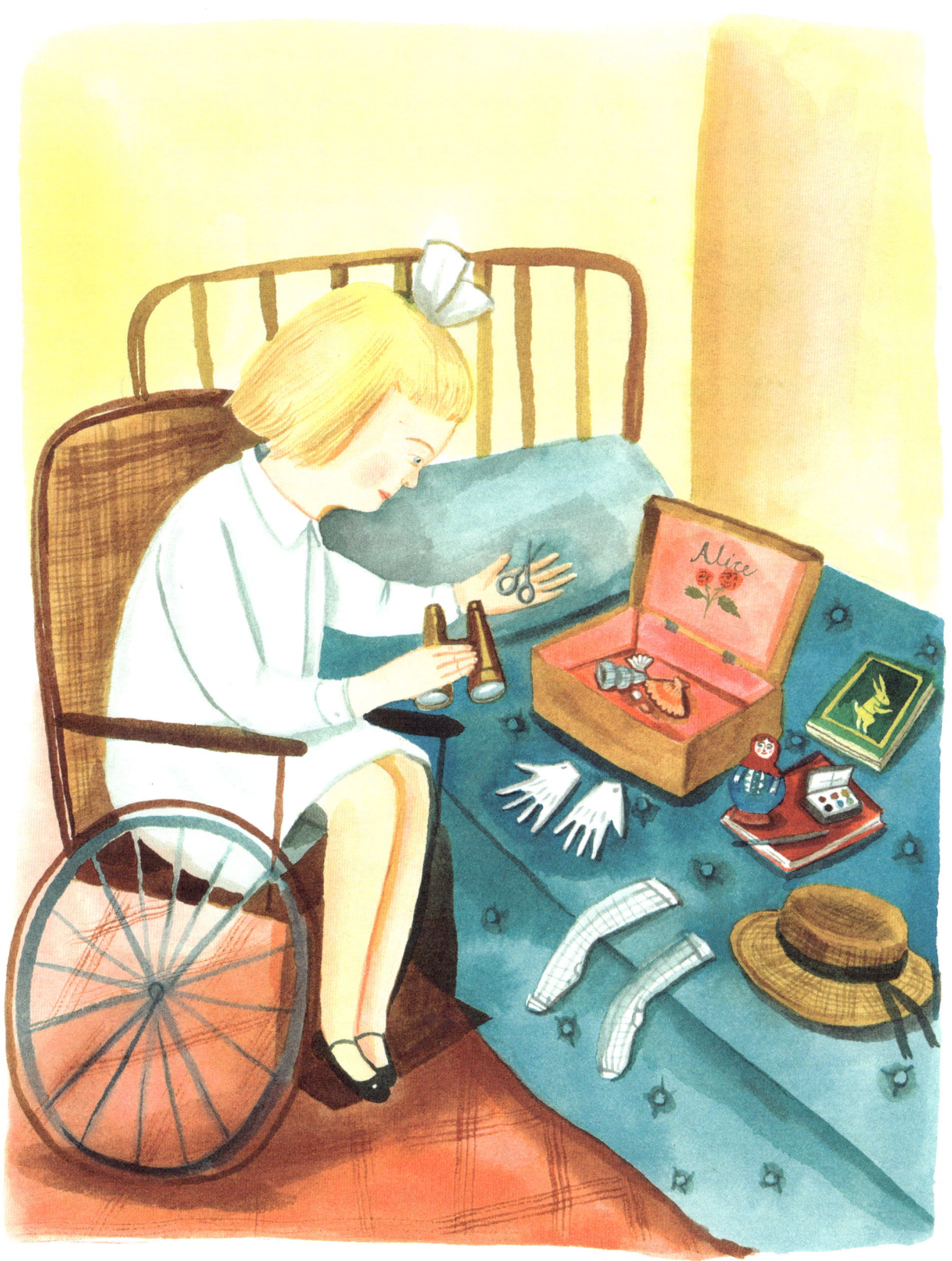

She spent the following days carefully packing her favorite things, with two new additions: a pair of binoculars from her father and some miniature scissors from her mother.

It wasn't long before she boarded a huge steamship with her nurse and waved goodbye to her mother, father, and sisters.

Just then, the wind caught her hat and it flew off into the water. Maybe her hat wanted to stay behind, but she was ready for what lay ahead!

At sea, Alice watched birds she had never seen before, as well as fish and seals, with her binoculars. She painted them all in her notebook.

When she finally arrived at her destination, she found herself in a stone hospital filled with children just like her.

There she spent many hours getting the sunlight her doctors thought would help her. She passed the time by painting pictures of the far-off mountains and learning French.

And she used her miniature scissors to make paper cutouts of the flowers she remembered from her family garden.

Sometimes, if she tried really hard, she could even hear the bird songs from home.

Her favorite present from her sisters was an owl they made from a walnut shell. When she missed them, she would take it out of her special tin box and write them stories about the walnut owl sailing away in a seashell boat to a faraway land.

Dear Mary and Peggy,
Once upon a time a little owl went to sea in a seashell pulled by fish

Over time, the sunlight, mountain air, and cheese did help Alice! Within a year, she returned home much stronger, and without a wheelchair. Instead, she wore special shoes that allowed her to keep up with her little sisters.

But since movement was still hard for her, she often sat at her easel and painted. She painted her family, birds, and flowers. She painted the view from her window, along with her dreams.

She loved looking at other people's paintings, too, and sometimes spent whole days in art museums. At one museum, she met another painter named Fuller.

Not long after, Alice and Fuller got married and had kids,

and then those kids had their own kids,

and one of those kids is me!

Now, Alice is my grandmother.

She's the one who taught me the names of flowers and birds and how to paint them with watercolors. But mostly, she has taught me how everyone has a story that is much bigger than the part you can see.

When I visit her and she brings out her special box, we pass each object back and forth.

Each one is a hint about who she was
before she became my grandmother.

She puts the owl in my hand and says, "Maybe you can add this to your own memory box!"

Nodding eagerly, I think about all the other treasures I will keep to help me tell my own story.